Marianna May and Nursey

by

Tomie dePaola

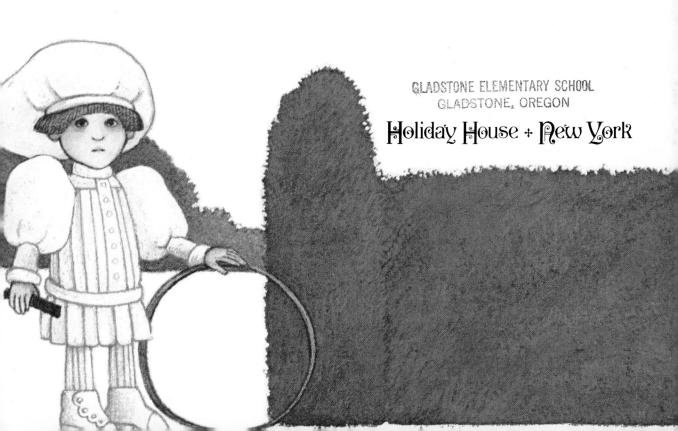

Holiday House + New York

For Tammy Grimes

24940

Library of Congress Cataloging in Publication Data

De Paola, Tomie.
   Marianna May and Nursey.

   Summary: A little rich girl is miserable
because she isn't allowed to do anything but
sit still and keep her white dress clean.
   [1. Cleanliness—Fiction] I. Title.
PZ7.D439Mar 1983   [E]   82-9364
ISBN 0-8234-0473-0

Marianna May was *very* rich.
So were Papa and Mama.

Papa and Mama were *always* very busy.
So Marianna May had a lady who took care of her.
The lady's name was Nursey.

Nursey *always* wore white, white, white.
And so did Marianna May. Especially in summer.

Nursey didn't like it

when Marianna May rolled in the grass,

made mud pies,

ate orange ice,

or strawberry ice cream.

Nursey didn't like it

when Marianna May painted picture

"Marianna May," said Nursey,
"sit nicely on the porch swing
and keep your white dress clean."

Even though Marianna May was very rich,
she was also very sad.

She liked rolling in the grass.

She liked making mud pies.

She liked orange ice and strawberry ice cream.

And she liked to paint pictures.

Mr. Talbot, who delivered the ice,
saw Marianna May sitting on the
porch swing day after day.
"How come you're always sittin', Missy?"
Mr. Talbot asked.

"Oh, Mr. Iceman, Nursey doesn't like it
  if I get my dress all dirty. She doesn't like it
  when I roll in the grass, or make mud pies,
  or eat orange ice and strawberry ice cream.
  And she especially doesn't like it
  when I paint pictures."

"Aw, poor Missy," said Mr. Talbot,
and he took the ice around back.

"Poor little Missy doesn't look like
she's having much fun this summer, Aggie,"
Mr. Talbot said to the cook's helper.

"Poor Miss Marianna May isn't having much fun,"
Aggie said to Jack the cook.

"Minnie," said Jack to Nursey
  (because that was Nursey's first name),
"Minnie, our little darlin' isn't having fun."

"Oh dear, Jack," said Nursey.
"Whatever shall we do?
  Every time she plays, her dresses get all dirty."

"And they are very hard to get sparkling,"
said Mrs. Jones, who did the laundry."

Nursey, Mrs. Jones, Jack the cook,
Aggie, and Mr. Talbot all sat
down and gazed out the window.

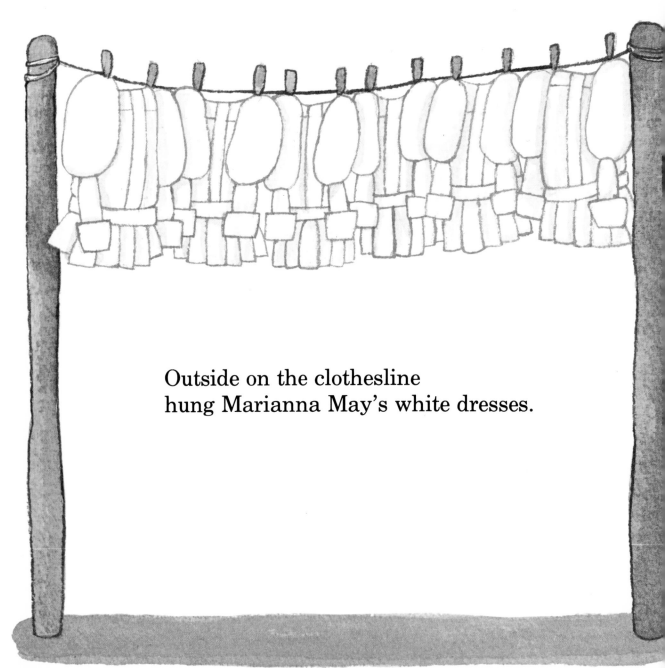

Outside on the clothesline
hung Marianna May's white dresses.

"I have it," said Mr. Talbot, jumping up.

He told everyone his idea.

The next day, when Aggie
came back from the grocery store,
Jack put big kettles of water on the stove.
Mrs. Jones got out all the laundry tubs, and
Nursey rolled up her sleeves.

They worked all afternoon.

For the rest of the summer,
Marianna May rolled in the grass.

She made mud pies.

She ate orange ice.

She ate strawberry ice cream.

And she painted pictures.

r mrs. Jones

for Jack

for Aggie

or mr. Talbot

for Nursey

for Papa and Mama

From that day on, there was only one time
when Marianna May wore white.